The Saddest King

Chris Wormell

A Tom Maschler Book

Jonathan Cape • London

There was once a country where the people were always happy.
Nothing ever made them sad, or cross, or miserable.

They would smile and laugh when the sun shone down . . .

. . . but they would also smile and laugh when it rained.

And even when the snow fell and the chattering of their teeth
was like an orchestra of rattles, they were still happy.

They were delighted when given bunches of beautiful flowers. But they were just as happy if the flowers were dead ones. And a bad apple seemed to please them as much as a box of chocolates.

If someone tripped and fell and landed on their head in that country, they'd most likely say, "What a lucky chance! I do think this bump suits me, don't you?" And if dinner was burnt they'd cry, "Brilliant! That's just the way we like it!"

Nothing ever made the people miserable. They were *always* happy – or at least they seemed to be.

But do you know what? They had no choice. Being unhappy was against the law in that country; being sad, or cross, or miserable was banned.

Happiness was compulsory, by order of the King. And the King, it was said, was the happiest person in the land.

Now, the people of that country might well have gone on being constantly happy, whatever happened to them, except that one day . . .

. . . a small boy broke the law.

He cried.

He cried in broad daylight, in the town square, before the great statue of the King, and no one could stop him. They tried to – they danced and sang and offered him buns and ice cream, but it was no good, they couldn't cheer him up.

"The King's guards will catch you if you don't laugh soon!" said an old woman. "And they'll take you off to the palace. They have a dungeon there where they *make* you laugh — they tie you up and tickle you with feathers!"

And sure enough, before very long, the King's guards
came and took the boy off to the palace.

The King was the most remarkable-looking person. He had the widest smile the boy had ever seen.

"Ho ho ho!" he chuckled. "What have we here – a miserable child? Impossible! *Everybody* is happy in this country!"

"No, they're not," said the boy, "they're just pretending. They're not really happy, not all the time."

"Yes, they are!" laughed the King. "Why would anyone want to be sad?"

"*I* want to be sad," said the boy.

"But . . . but . . . *why*?" demanded the King.

"Because of my dog," said the boy.
"I had a dog and he was the best dog
in the world.

"I loved my dog and he
loved me, and he could do tricks;
he was really clever, my dog.
He was my best friend.

"But one day he got ill and then
he died. That's why I'm sad sometimes.
And I don't care what you do to me. I'll
still be sad because I *want* to be sad."

The King did nothing. He just looked down at the boy with his enormous fixed smile. Then he began to make a strange noise. It sounded like sobbing . . . which was odd, because he was still grinning from ear to ear.

The boy was puzzled, and looked closely at the King. Then he cried, "Why, you're wearing a mask!" And before the King could move, he reached up and pulled it away.

Behind the mask was the saddest face the boy had ever seen. Great tears rolled down the King's cheeks.

"I'm not a happy king," he sobbed.

"For I once had a dog, too, and he was *my* best friend. He was my only friend. Everybody pretends to like me, because I'm the King, but only my dog really loved me. He used to chew my slippers to shreds, and pull off all my bedclothes, and even steal the food from my dinner plate! Only my dog was true.

"And when he grew old and died, I was filled with sadness.
No one dared laugh or even smile in my presence and the
palace became a place of misery. I wanted it to be a happy
place again, so I made happiness compulsory. And soon I
was pretending, just like everybody else."

"It's all right to be sad," said the boy. "Everybody needs to be sad sometimes. When I feel sad I think about my dog and I remember all the clever tricks he could do."

At this, the King looked up and said,
"My dog would dance on his hind
legs when I played the fiddle."

"Wow!" said the boy.
"That's clever! My dog could do
somersaults through a hoop!"

"Could he?" cried the King. "Mine, I'm
afraid, was rather naughty – he'd steal sausages
from the palace kitchens."

"My dog was a terror!" cried the boy. "He once pulled all the clothes from my mum's washing line and rolled them in the mud."

"Ha! He sounds wonderful!" laughed the King, and soon they were both laughing, remembering happy times.

They cried a bit, too.

"You have to be the way you feel," said the boy.

"Of course you do," agreed the King. "I've been a fool!"

And right then and there, he tore up the special order that made happiness compulsory. From that day on, everyone was allowed to feel just the way they wanted to.

And do you know what happened then?

Everybody in the land had a really good cry . . .

because they hadn't had one for years!

For Arran and George

THE SADDEST KING
A JONATHAN CAPE BOOK 978 0 224 07045 4

Published in Great Britain by Jonathan Cape,
an imprint of Random House Children's Books

This edition published 2007

1 3 5 7 9 10 8 6 4 2

RANDOM HOUSE CHILDREN'S BOOKS
61–63 Uxbridge Road, London W5 5SA
A division of The Random House Group Ltd

RANDOM HOUSE AUSTRALIA (PTY) LTD
20 Alfred Street, Milsons Point, Sydney,
New South Wales 2061, Australia

RANDOM HOUSE NEW ZEALAND LTD
18 Poland Road, Glenfield, Auckland 10, New Zealand

RANDOM HOUSE (PTY) LTD
Isle of Houghton, Corner Boundary Road & Carse O'Gowrie,
Houghton 2198, South Africa

RANDOM HOUSE INDIA PVT LTD
301 World Trade Tower, Hotel Intercontinental Grand Complex,
Barakhamba Lane, New Delhi 110001, India

THE RANDOM HOUSE GROUP Limited Reg. No. 954009
www.**kids**at**randomhouse**.co.uk

A CIP catalogue record for this book is available from the British Library.

Printed and bound in Singapore.